INTRODUCTION

I'VE ALWAYS been fascinated by spiders. I used to collect them when I was younger. I'd spend hours rooting through the dusty old shed at the bottom of our garden, hunting the cobwebs for lurking eight-legged predators. When I found one, I'd bring it in and let it loose in my bedroom.

It used to drive my mum mad!

Usually, the spider would slip away after no more than a day or two, never to be seen again, but sometimes they hung around longer. I had one who made a cobweb above my bed and stood sentry for almost a month. Going to sleep, I used to imagine the spider creeping down, crawling into my mouth, sliding down my throat and laying loads of eggs in my belly. The baby spiders would hatch after a while and eat me alive, from the inside out.

I loved being scared when I was little.

When I was nine, my mum and dad gave me a small tarantula. It wasn't poisonous or very big, but it was the greatest gift I'd ever received. I played with that spider almost every waking hour of the day. Gave it all sorts of treats: flies and cockroaches and tiny worms. Spoilt it rotten.

Then, one day, I did something stupid. I'd been watching a cartoon in which one of the characters was sucked up by a vacuum cleaner. No harm came to him. He squeezed out of the bag, dusty and dirty and mad as hell. It was very funny.

So funny, I tried it myself. With the tarantula.

Needless to say, things didn't happen quite like they did in the cartoon. The spider was ripped to pieces. I cried a lot, but it

was too late for tears. My pet was dead, it was my fault, and there was nothing I could do about it.

My parents nearly hollered the roof down when they found out what I'd done – the tarantula had cost quite a bit of money. They said I was an irresponsible fool, and from that day on they never again let me have a pet, not even an ordinary garden spider.

I started with that tale from the past for two reasons. One will become obvious as this book unfolds. The other reason is:

This is a true story.

I don't expect you to believe me – I wouldn't believe it myself if I hadn't lived it – but it is. Everything I describe in this book happened, just as I tell it.

The thing about real life is, when you do something stupid, it normally costs you. In books, the heroes can make as many mistakes as they like. It doesn't matter what they do, because everything comes good at the end. They'll beat the bad guys and put things right and everything ends up hunky-dory.

In real life, vacuum cleaners kill spiders. If you cross a busy road without looking, you get whacked by a car. If you fall out of a tree, you break some bones.

Real life's nasty. It's cruel. It doesn't care about heroes and happy endings and the way things should be. In real life, bad things happen. People die. Fights are lost. Evil often wins.

I just wanted to make that clear before I began.

One more thing: my name isn't really Darren Shan. Everything's true in this book, *except* for names. I've had to change them because... well, by the time you get to the end, you'll understand.

I haven't used *any* real names, not mine, my sister's, my friends or teachers. Nobody's. I'm not even going to tell you the name of my town or country. I daren't.

Anyway, that's enough of an introduction. If you're ready, let's begin. If this was a made-up story, it would begin at night, with a storm blowing and owls hooting and rattling noises under the bed. But this is a real story, so I have to begin where it really started.

It started in a toilet.

CHAPTER ONE

I WAS in the toilet at school, sitting down, humming a song. I had my trousers on. I'd come in near the end of English class, feeling sick. My teacher, Mr Dalton, is great about things like that. He's smart and knows when you're faking and when you're being serious. He took one look at me when I raised my hand and said I was ill, then nodded his head and told me to make for the toilet.

"Throw up whatever's bugging you, Darren," he said, "then get your behind back in here."

I wish every teacher was as understanding as Mr Dalton.

In the end, I didn't get sick, but still felt queasy, so I stayed on the toilet. I heard the bell ring for the end of class and everybody came rushing out on their lunch break. I wanted to join them but knew Mr Dalton would give out if he saw me in the yard so soon. He doesn't get mad if you trick him but he goes quiet and won't speak to you for ages, and that's almost worse than being shouted at.

So, there I was, humming, watching my watch, waiting. Then I heard someone calling my name.

"Darren! Hey, Darren! Have you fallen in or what?"

I grinned. It was Steve Leopard, my best friend. Steve's real surname was Leonard, but everyone called him Steve Leopard. And not just because the names sound alike. Steve used to be what my mum calls "a wild child". He raised hell wherever he went, got into fights, stole in shops. One day – he was still in a pushchair – he found a sharp stick and prodded passing women with it (no prizes for guessing where he stuck it!).

He was feared and despised everywhere he went. But not by me. I've been his best friend since Montessori, when we first met. My mum says I was drawn to his wildness, but I just thought he was a great guy to be with. He had a fierce temper, and threw scary tantrums when he lost it, but I simply ran away when that happened and came back again once he'd calmed down.

Steve's reputation had softened over the years – his mum took him to see a lot of good counsellors who taught him how to control himself – but he was still a minor legend in the schoolyard and not someone you messed with, even if you were bigger and older than him.

"Hey, Steve," I called back. "I'm in here." I hit the door so he'd know which one I was behind.

He hurried over and I opened the door. He smiled when he saw me sitting down with my trousers on. "Did you puke?" he asked.

"No," I said.

"Do you think you're gonna?"

"Maybe," I said. Then I leaned forward all of a sudden and made a sick noise. Bluurgh! But Steve Leopard knew me too well to be fooled.

"Give my boots a polish while you're down there," he said, and laughed when I pretended to spit on his shoes and rub them with a sheet of toilet paper.

"Did I miss anything in class?" I asked, sitting up.

"Nah," he said. "The usual crap."

"Did you do your history homework?" I asked.

"It doesn't have to be done until tomorrow, does it?" he asked, getting worried. Steve's always forgetting about homework.

"The day after tomorrow," I told him.

"Oh," he said, relaxing. "Even better. I thought... "

He stopped and frowned. "Hold on," he said. "Today's Thursday. The day after tomorrow would be... "

"Got you!" I yelled, punching him on the shoulder.

"Ow!" he shouted. "That hurt." He rubbed his arm but I could tell he wasn't really hurt. "Are you coming out?" he asked then.

"I thought I'd stay in here and admire the view," I said, leaning back on the toilet seat.

"Quit messing," he said. "We were five-one down when I came in. We're probably six or seven down now. We need you." He was talking about football. We play a game every lunchtime. My team normally wins but we'd lost a lot of our best players. Dave Morgan broke his leg. Sam White transferred to another school when his family moved. And Danny Curtain had stopped playing football in order to spend lunch hanging out with Sheila Leigh, the girl he fancies. Idiot!

I'm our best full-forward. There are better defenders and midfielders, and Tommy Jones is the best goalkeeper in the whole school. But I'm the only one who can stand up front and score four or five times a day without fail.

"OK," I said, standing. "I'll save you. I've scored a hat trick every day this week. It would be a pity to stop now."

We passed the older guys — smoking around the sinks as usual — and hurried to my locker so I could change into my trainers. I used to have a great pair, which I won in a writing competition. But the laces snapped a few months ago and the rubber along the sides started to fall off. And then my feet grew! The pair I have now are OK but they're not the same.

We were eight-three down when I got on the pitch. It wasn't a real pitch, just a long stretch of yard with painted goal posts at either end. Whoever painted them was a right idiot. He put the crossbar too high at one end and too low at the other!

"Never fear, Hotshot Shan is here!" I shouted as I ran onto the pitch. A lot of players laughed or groaned, but I could see my team mates picking up and our opponents growing worried.

I made a great start and scored two goals inside a minute. It looked like we might come back to draw or win. But time ran out. If I'd arrived earlier we'd have been OK but the bell rang just as I was hitting my stride, so we lost nine-seven.

As we were leaving the pitch, Alan Morris ran into the yard, panting and red-faced. They're my three best friends: Steve Leopard, Tommy Jones and Alan Morris. We must be the oddest four people in the whole world, because only one of us – Steve – has a nickname.

"Look what I found!" Alan yelled, waving a soggy piece of paper around under our noses.

"What is it?" Tommy asked, trying to grab it.

"It's— " Alan began, but stopped when Mr Dalton shouted at us.

"You four! Inside!" he roared.

"We're coming, Mr Dalton!" Steve roared back. Steve is Mr Dalton's favourite and gets away with stuff that the rest of us couldn't do. Like when he uses swear words sometimes in his stories. If I put in some of the words Steve has, I'd have been kicked out long ago.

But Mr Dalton has a soft spot for Steve, because he's special. Sometimes he's brilliant in class and gets everything right, while other times he can't even spell his own name. Mr Dalton says he's a bit of an *idiot savant*, which mean he's a stupid genius!

Anyway, even though he's Mr Dalton's pet, not even Steve can get away with turning up late for class. So whatever Alan had, it would have to wait. We trudged back to class, sweaty and tired after the game, and began our next lesson.

Little did I know that Alan's mysterious piece of paper was to change my life forever. For the worse!

DO YOU THINK THAT'S WEIRD? IT SEEMS LIKE THE ONLY PERSON WHO UNDERSTANDS ME IS MY BEST FRIEND, STEVE.

MY NAME IS DARREN SHAN.

MY FAVOUR-ITE THINGS IN THE WORLD ARE...

EVERY-ONE ELSE JUST GETS CREEPED OUT, BUT I DON'T CARE!

...SPIDERS!

CHAPTER 1: DARREN AND STEVE

THERE'S NO ONE I'D RATHER HANG AROUND WITH!

PERHAPS IT WAS DESTINY THAT DREW US TO THAT CIRCUS.

YES, PER-HAPS...

PAPER: CIRQUE DU FREAK

CHAPTER 1:
DARREN AND STEVE

FRIDAY OF THE DEATH

YEAH, JUST A FEW!

BLOOD VAMPIRE

WOW, DID YOU GET SOME NEW POSTERS?

THE ONE

ARE YOU KEEPING ANY SPIDERS AGAIN?

AND YOUR OBSESSION WITH SPIDERS IS JUST AS BAD!

TSUTSUUU (DROOP)

YOU SURE DO LOVE YOUR HORROR STUFF...

NOT AFTER THAT TIME I SUCKED THE TARANTULA THEY BOUGHT ME INTO THE VACUUM CLEANER.

NO, MUM AND DAD WON'T LET ME ANYMORE.

WUNDER WHAT KIND IT IS. AN ORB-WEAVER, MAYBE?

A SPI-DER!!

PAA (PZOW)

WOW!

NO, IT CAN BE ANY-THING...

SAY, YOU KNOW HOW YOU HAVE TO USE A STAKE TO KILL A VAMPIRE...?

DOES THE STAKE HAVE TO BE MADE OUT OF WOOD?

14

SFX: GAAAA (RAWRRR)

WAIT,
WHAT'S
...

...

KIN KON KAN KON
(DING DONG
BING BONG)

AND THEREFORE, ONCE WORLD WAR II HAD EFFECTIVELY CONCLUDED AROUND THE GLOBE...

...THE TOTAL NUMBER OF CASUALTIES WAS MORE THAN 72 MILLION.

YOU'VE REALLY GOT A THIRST FOR VIOLENCE, DON'T YOU, STEVE?

I'LL GET PAID TO FIGHT AND TRAVEL AROUND THE WORLD!

WARS ARE COOL. WHEN I GROW UP, I'M GOING TO BE A MERCENARY!

HEY, DARREN!

WHAT'S THAT?

THAT'S THE BEST PART! IT'S A BATTLE FOR YOUR LIFE!

GOSO (RUSTLE) GOSO

GO OFF TO WAR, AND YOU'LL WIND UP DEAD.

SFX: DADADA (RATTA-RATTA-RATTA)

KUSHA (SKSHH)

HA HA HA.

18

HMM...

HEY!

OH, WELL, I WAS...

ヒョイ (HYOI) (YANK)

OOOH!

THAT SOUNDS NEAT! WHERE'D YOU GET THIS?

PIRA (FLAP)

ヒラ

AND BY "FREAK," I'M GUESSING THEY MEAN FREAKS OF NATURE.

"CIRQUE" IS FRENCH FOR CIRCUS.

CIRQUE DU FREAK, THE CIR-CUS OF FREAKS...

WEIRD GUY?

IT'S A CIRCUS!

SOME WEIRD GUY GAVE IT TO ME ON THE WAY HOME FROM STEVE'S HOUSE LAST NIGHT.

THIS LOOKS REALLY COOL!

AND IT'S ONLY RUNNING UNTIL THIS TUESDAY, DARREN!

FLYER: CIRQUE DU FREAK /
LIMITED SHOWING: 9/8 — 15/9 /
£15 PER PERSON

SEE:

SIVE AND
SEERSA—
THE TWISTING
TWINS

THE SNAKE-BOY

THE WOLF-MAN

GERTHA TEETH

LARTEN
CREPSLEY AND
HIS PERFORMING
SPIDER—
MADAM OCTA

ALEXANDER RIBS

THE BEARDED
LADY

HANS HANDS

RHAMUS
TWOBELLIES—
WORLD'S
FATTEST MAN

WARNING!!
SOME RESTRICTIONS
APPLY! NOT FOR THE
FAINTHEARTED!!

AHA! I SEE, THEN ...

I WAS GOING TO ASK YOU ABOUT IT LATER, AT THE END OF CLASS.

I THOUGHT IT LOOKED INTERESTING, SO I PICKED IT UP.

YOURS, STEVE?

SIT DOWN, STEVE, DARREN.

TON (TAP) TON

THAT'S DIFFERENT. NOTHING WRONG WITH AN INQUISITIVE MIND.

THE CON MEN PUT THESE POOR PEOPLE ON DISPLAY AND CALLED THEM FREAKS.

A PERSON WITH THREE ARMS OR TWO NOSES.

SOMEONE WHO DOESN'T LOOK ORDINARY.

SIR, WHAT'S "MALFORMED" MEAN?

GREEDY CON MEN CRAMMED MALFORMED PEOPLE IN CAGES AND...

LONG AGO, THERE USED TO BE REAL FREAK SHOWS.

AND THESE POOR PEOPLE WERE NO DIFFERENT FROM YOU OR ME, EXCEPT IN LOOKS.

HOW AWFUL!

THAT'S CRUEL!

THEY CHARGED THE PUBLIC TO STARE AT THEM AND INVITED THEM TO LAUGH AND TEASE.

QUESTION!

KIN KON
(DING DONG)

WE'RE GOING!

HI, MUM!

WELCOME HOME, DARREN.

POI (TOSS)
ポイ!!

AND REMEMBER TO TAKE YOUR BATH!

SORRY, MUM!

トタタ
TOTATA (CTROMP)

DON'T TOSS YOUR BAG ON THE FLOOR!

HEY! DAR-REN!

24

THIS IS GONNA BE THE COOLEST THING EVER!

KYU (SKRK)

ZABAA (SPLOSH)

FLYER: RHAMUS TWOBELLIES—WORLD'S FATTEST MAN

I SAID I WANTED IT FOR MY BEDROOM WALL.

HUH?

WHAT DID YOU SAY TO HIM?

BUT HEY, AT LEAST YOU CONVINCED HIM TO GIVE THE FLYER BACK!

TOO BAD MR. DALTON SNIPPED OFF THE ADDRESS.

ADULTS WILL DO ANYTHING AS LONG AS YOU BUTTER THEM UP!

GAA (GRARR)

HE'S WAY TOO SOFT ON YOU!

ARE YOU KIDDING ME?

IT'S £15 FOR A TICKET, RIGHT?

WHAT ABOUT THE MONEY?

YEAH!! THERE'S NO WAY WE'RE MISSING THIS!!!

SO WHAT'S THE PLAN? ARE WE ALL GOING?

OUR HERO!

HA-HA-HA-HA

STEVE THE GREAT!

ALL MEMORIZED!

OOOO (OOOH)

OH YEAH!

WHAT ABOUT THE DIRECTIONS?

WHY DO YOU THINK WE PLAY FOOTBALL FOR MONEY?

WE'VE GOT £60 JUST FROM THAT!

SEE YOU TOMORROW! HOPE YOU'RE EXCITED!

BISHI (GRIN)

I'LL SNEAK OUT AT NIGHT AND BUY US THE TICKETS!

CIRQUE DU FREAK...

FLYER: PERFORMING SPIDER — MADAM OCTA

...HAS TO BE THE SPIDER...

きょくげい 曲芸グモ

THE ONE I WANT TO SEE THE MOST...

HE WANTS TO GO MOST OF ALL!

"YOU'D HAVE TO BE TWISTED TO WANT TO GO TO A FREAK SHOW," INDEED!

GOSHI (RUB)

GOSHI

MOGU
(MUNCH)
MOGU
モグ モグ

GA
(CHOMP)

GA

WHAT A
GOOD BOY!
HE EVEN
TOOK HIS
DISHES TO
THE SINK.

JIIII
(STARE)
じ〜

ALL
DONE!
THAT
WAS
GOOD.

NOTH-
ING'S
WRONG.

WHAT'S
WRONG
WITH YOU?
YOU'RE HIDING
SOMETHING!

I DON'T
KNOW.
LET'S HOPE
HE DOESN'T
GET ANY
STRANGER!

WHY IS
DARREN
ACTING SO
STRANGE?

ピンポォン

PINPONNN
(DING-
DONGGG)

SMASH

28

OOOH!!

HUH?

THAT'S ALL OF THEM?

AS YOU CAN SEE, I'VE GOT THE TICKETS!

FIRST, THE GOOD NEWS.

YEP, THAT'S THE BAD NEWS.

TICKETS: CIRQUE DU FREAK

HUH...?

THESE WERE THE ONLY TWO I COULD GET.

...WHO GETS THE TICKETS?

S-SO...

SOLD OUT!?

IN FACT, THESE WERE THE LAST TWO TICKETS BEFORE THE SHOW WAS SOLD OUT.

YOU'VE GOTTA BE KIDDING ME!

GAAN (DONGG)

I CAN'T BELIEVE IT!

YESSSSS!

よっしゃあぁ

GOAAAAL!!

HA HA HA HA!

TICKET: CIRQUE DU FREAK

YEAH, I CONVINCED THEM I WAS STAYING AT YOUR HOUSE!

WERE YOUR PARENTS OKAY WITH IT?

THANKS FOR WAITING!

OH NO!

DAMN. IT'S MR. DALTON AND THE POLICE.

THEY'RE STAKING THE PLACE OUT TO MAKE SURE NO CHILDREN ARE GOING.

CHI (TSK)

HE MUST HAVE USED THE MAP ON THE FLYER.

GUWAA (GRARRG)

PUKUU (PSHHT)

...

HOW DARE YOU HAND THESE OUT!

AND TO CHILDREN!

HEY, CHECK IT OUT!

AFTER ALL OUR HARD WORK...

HOW CAN THIS BE HAPPENING?

38

GOOOO, (WHOOOOSH)

⁉️

VERY WELL.

AAAH.

HMM, YOU ARE VERY LATE, BOYS.

TICKETS, PLEASE.

MMMMM.

OH!

? ?

SFX: GOKUKU (GULP)

SFX: PAKU (CHOMP)

SO WE WILL MAKE AN EXCEPTION.

NORMALLY, WE DON'T WELCOME CHILDREN, BUT I CAN SEE YOU ARE TWO FINE, COURAGEOUS YOUNG MEN.

SHAAAA (SHHHK)

YOU MAY GO IN NOW.

SUUU (SHHH)

THEY'RE STARTING!

I RECKON HE WAS A REAL MIND-READER.

WOW, THAT WAS JUST LIKE WHAT THAT GUY DID!

SFX: DOK! (BA-BUMP) DOK!

SO, STEVE, I WAS THINKING...

I BET YOU ANY-THING YOU LIKE THEY DON'T SELL POPCORN.

...HOME OF THE WORLD'S MOST REMARK-ABLE HUMAN BEINGS!

...WELCOME TO THE CIRQUE DU FREAK...

BA (FLIK)

LADIES AND GEN-TLEMEN...

SFX: WAA (RAHH)   SFX: KUN (SNIFF)

GURURURU
(GRRRRR)

GRAWWWR...

AWOOOOOO!!

BIRI
(BZZ)

BIRI

EEK!

ZUDODODO
(ZDOOMM)

NOOOO!!

GAAAA
(RAWWWR)

47

MUSHI
(GRSSHT)

!! AAH!

EEK!

SFX: GONYO (WHISPER) GONYO

EEEH!

DARAN...
(BLONGG)

AHH!

EEK!

TATA
(TSHH)

KIRA
(KLING)

SFX: PARA (SPRINKLE) PARA

SHA
(SHK)

SHA

SHA

T-THAT'S THE GUY WHO LIFTED MR. DALTON OFF HIS FEET...

SFX: BURU (SHIVER) BURU

OH, GOOD...

OOOH!

I-IT'S MOVING! I CAN MOVE MY FINGERS!

TH-THANK YOU...

SUU
(SHFFF)

PUTSUN
(SNAP)

BAAN
(TA-DAA)

ZA
(ZSHH)

Mr. Crepsley...

...And his performing spider... ...Madam Octaaa!

ABOUT TIME!

NIYA (SMIRK)

ZOWA, CZSHHH

STE I

STEVE!

SHH!

?

SFX: GATA (SHIVER) GATA

HEY, STEVE...

HUH? HE LOOKS A LOT LIKE THE GUY WHO GAVE ME THE FLYER.

I'M JUST FINE, STUPID.

HUH?

...

DID THE SPIDER SCARE YOU?

LOOK AT *YOUR* PALE FACE!

ARE YOU...OKAY? FEELING BAD?

GOSHI (RUB)

STEVE?

PACHI

PACHI (CLAP)

PACHI

PACHI

PACHI

PACHI

PACHI

PACHI

PACHI

PACHI

MR. TALL!

IT WAS FABU-LOUS!

WELL, BOYS, DID YOU ENJOY THE SHOW?

(ZORO (MUTTER))

ZORO

HO-HO! YOU'RE A TOUGH PAIR.

A LITTLE, BUT NO MORE THAN ANYBODY ELSE.

YOU WEREN'T SCARED?

GO BACK BY YOUR-SELF.

THAT WAS SO MUCH FUN!

DAR-REN.

YEAH?

I MADE SURE TO GET PLENTY OF SOUVENIRS!

THEY'LL ALL BE AMAZED!

66

WHAT?

DOWA (THUDD)

STEVE!!

WHY NOT, STEVE!?

I'M NOT COMING! I'M STAYING!

YOU HEARD!

DODODODO

DODODODODO (DMM)

I HAVE TO TELL YOU...

YOU KNOW, DARREN?

...THAT THIS CIRCUS WOULD CHANGE MY LIFE FOREVER, AND FOR THE WORSE.

AT THIS MOMENT, I COULD NEVER HAVE DREAMED ...

THE HAND OF DESTINY HAD JUST BEGUN TO TICK.

I HAD ALWAYS BELIEVED THAT STEVE AND I...

...WERE FRIENDS FOR LIFE.

CHAPTER 2:
A DANGEROUS GAME

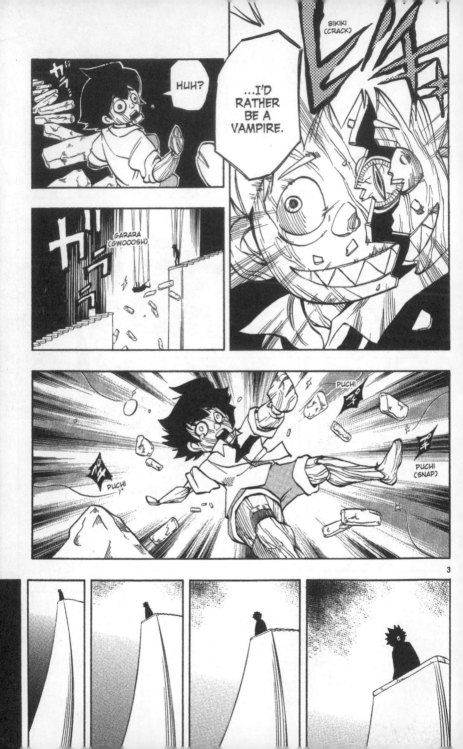

SFX: HAA (HUFF) HAA

AAAH!!

GABA
(LURCH)

DARREN! WHAT TOOK YOU SO LONG TO SHOW UP?

TOMMY, ALAN.

!

HOW'D IT GO, THEN!? WE NEED DETAILS!

I KNOW! AND STEVE ISN'T HERE YET EITHER.

WHAT ABOUT YOU, TOMMY?

I COULDN'T SLEEP A WINK LAST NIGHT!

SFX: KIN KON (DING DONG)

BAKI (CRAK)

SU (SHH)

COME HERE.

I WILL HAVE TO TEST YOU FIRST.

YOU HAVE THOUGHT THIS THROUGH?

KOKU (NOD)

YOU ARE CERTAIN IT IS WHAT YOU WANT?

STOP! DON'T DO IT, STEVE!

ZUBU (SLURP)

AAAGH!!

GOTTA SAVE...

I HAVE TO MOVE! I CAN'T BE SCARED!

BUT IF I DON'T SAVE HIM, WHO WILL?

SFX: ZUZUZU (SHUDDER)

I'M SCARED!

I'M SO SCARED, I CAN'T MOVE!

SFX: POTA (DRIP) POTA

I RAN AWAY. I LEFT STEVE BEHIND AND RAN FOR MY LIFE...

SFX: GACHA (CLICK)

I'M THE WORST!

!?

WELL, AREN'T WE LATE!

MOST OF THEIR PREY IS SMALL INSECTS.

THEY DON'T ACTUALLY NEED IT.

ペラ
PERA

ペラ
PERA (BLAH)

YOU KNOW HOW SOME SPIDERS HAVE DEADLY POISON? LIKE TARANTULAS!

...COOL! POWERFUL! SMART!

THEY'LL EVEN ATTACK HUMANS IF THEY SENSE DANGER!

BUT SPIDERS KEEP THAT UN-NECESSARILY POWERFUL POISON...

...IN CASE THEY FIGHT ANIMALS LARGER THAN THEM!

?

OF COURSE, VERY FEW HAVE POISON STRONG ENOUGH TO KILL A HUMAN...

THEY'RE FEARLESS CHALLENG-ERS!

YOU COULD SEARCH THE WORLD OVER AND NEVER FIND A BETTER SPIDER!

I BET MADAM OCTA COULD KILL ANY HUMAN WITH HER POISON!

ぽわ
ぁん
POWAAN (GLOWWW)

THAT'S THE THING!

WAIT A SECOND! DIDN'T MADAM OCTA KILL A GOAT THAT WAS LARGER THAN A HUMAN?

LIKE WHEN MR. CREPSLEY HAD HER IN HIS MOUTH!

BUT YOU SAID THAT OTHER PEOPLE CONTROLLED MADAM OCTA TOO.

CREPSLEY MUST HAVE BEEN CASTING A SPELL WITH THAT FLUTE!

DIDN'T I TELL YOU? HIS FLUTE!

HOW DO YOU THINK HE CONTROLLED THE SPIDER?

OH, YEAH.

IT WAS TELEPATHY.

THAT'S HOW THEY CONTROLLED THE SPIDER, WITH THEIR MINDS.

THE FLUTES ARE JUST FOR SHOW...

IT'S LIKE WHEN YOU BOTH SAY THE SAME THING AT THE SAME TIME, OR YOU MAKE EYE CONTACT WHEN PLAYING FOOTBALL.

EVERYONE HAS THAT ABILITY TO SOME DEGREE, WHETHER LARGE OR SMALL.

TELEPATHY IS WHEN YOU CAN READ SOMEBODY ELSE'S MIND, OR SEND THEM THOUGHTS WITHOUT SPEAKING.

TELE- PATHY?

AND HERE I AM...

ゴ......
GOKU
(GULP)

IT'S STILL EARLY...

THE FREAKS MIGHT STILL BE SLEEPING...

SFX: GI (CREAK)

I'LL FORGET SHE EVER EXISTED!

...I'LL GIVE UP ON MADAM OCTA.

IF THIS DOOR IS LOCKED...

92

UH.

KIIIII (CREEEEAK)

IT'S OPEN!!

OOOO (WHOOOSH)

SFX: DO DO (BA-DUMP)

SFX: BATAN (THUMP)

NO! FORGET HER!

I HAVE TO GIVE UP ON THE SPIDER AND JUST GO HOME!

ARE YOU AFRAID, DARREN?

DIDN'T YOU WANT TO SEE MADAM OCTA?

MAYBE I SHOULD LEAVE.

KURU (SPIN)

GACHI

GACHI
(SHIVER)

WHAT THE HELL AM I DOING!?

OH, COME ON!

TA
(TMP)

IF THEY'RE NOT HERE, IT'S TIME TO GIVE UP AND GO HOME, DARREN!

THE FREAKS MIGHT HAVE ALREADY LEFT FOR THE NEXT TOWN.

YES- TERDAY WAS THE FINAL PERFOR- MANCE.

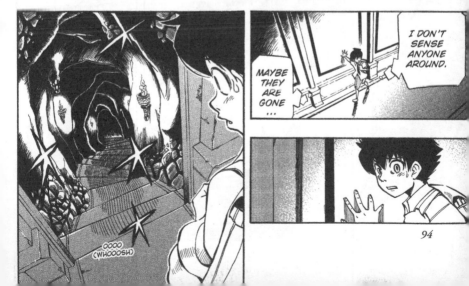

MAYBE THEY ARE GONE...

I DON'T SENSE ANYONE AROUND.

OOOO (WHOOOSH)

94

DO
(BA-DUMP)

BA
(WHOOSH)

SFX: MOZO (RUSTLE) MOZO

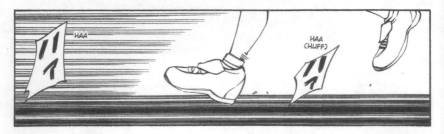

SFX: NIKO (GRIN) NIKO

GABU MUSHA
(GRRK MUNCH)

IT'S FEEDING TIME SOON.

HANG ON, GIRL.

MOZO

MOZO
(RUSTLE)

JUST LIKE STEVE SAID, IT TURNED OUT THAT ANYONE COULD CONTROL MADAM OCTA!

AT FIRST, I HAD SEVERAL CLOSE SHAVES, BUT ONCE I GOT THE HANG OF IT, SHE WAS MINE!

THE THEATRE WAS DESERTED ONCE MORE.

AFTER A WHILE, I STOPPED WORRYING.

THE CIRQUE DU FREAK HAD MOVED ON TO ITS NEXT DESTINATION.

STILL, I KEPT A CROSS CLOSE AT HAND!

GACHI (SHIVER)

GACHI

I WAS TERRIFIED OF CREPSLEY COMING AFTER ME AT ANY MOMENT.

MADAM OCTA BELONGED TO ME!

YEEE...

YES!!

YES! I DID IT! THE LETTER HAD WORKED!

FOR A SPECIAL TREAT, A PIECE OF PIZZA!

MY JOURNAL'S NEARLY FULL OF ENTRIES!

I BOUGHT A PIZZA TO CELEBRATE, AND SHE GOBBLED IT DOWN!

BAKU

BAKU (CHOMP)

HAA HAA

STEVE...

HAA (CHUFF)

HAA

HAA

YOU WON'T TALK TO ME, AND YOU WON'T MEET MY GAZE! WHAT'S GOING ON?

DON'T PLAY DUMB! YOU'VE BEEN STEERING CLEAR OF ME THESE PAST TWO WEEKS.

WHY HAVE YOU BEEN AVOIDING ME?

WHAT DO YOU MEAN?

PA
(FLIK)

THAT SORRY WAS OVER THE TOP.

GEHO
(COUGH)
GEHO

ARE EVEN YOU SAYING I'M EVIL, NOW!?

SFX: GA (GRRK)

YOU'RE HURT-ING ME... STEVE...

SFX: GUGU (GRRG)

YOU'RE MY BEST FRIEND, DARREN ...

IF YOU BREAK UP OUR FRIENDSHIP... I DON'T KNOW WHAT I'LL DO...

I-I JUST DON'T KNOW WHAT TO DO ANYMORE...

WAH!

WAH!

W-WHEN I THOUGHT ABOUT YOU... BECOMING A V-VAMPIRE ...

I WAS SCARED TOO!

HI
HIKKU
(CHIC HIC)

WAAHHH!

BOO HOO HOO!

SFX: ZORO (CREEP)

SFX: FURI (WIGGLE) FURI

DO (WHAM)

BIKU (TWIK)

STOP!

SFX: KASA (SCUTTLE)

SHAA (HSSS)

116

TOON (ZOOSHH)

SFX: MOZO (RUSTLE)

NIYARI (NYEH HEH)

HUH...?

TELL MUM TO CALL AN AMBULANCE, ANNIE.

HENA... (PLOP)

SU (SHH)

GYU (SQUEEZE)

SFX: PIIPOO (WEE-OOH) PIIPOO

HURRY!

I-I'M GOING!

KURU
(SPIN)

DA (DSHH)

HAA

HAA
(CHUFF)

BASA
(FLAP)

BASA

HAH. WHY SO ANGRY?

FUWA (FWUSH)

CREPSLEY!!

HAVE YOU COME TO TAKE MADAM OCTA "BACK"?

MADAM OCTA SAYS SHE LIKED YOU QUITE A BIT...

THAT IS A RUDE THING TO SAY ABOUT A LADY.

I NEVER WANT TO SEE THAT MONSTER AGAIN!

SFX: GATA (SHIVER) GATA

PLEASE!

I WANT YOU TO MAKE HIM BETTER!

A NASTY BUSINESS.

THE ONE KNOWN AS "STEVE LEOPARD"...

SHE BIT STEVE LEONARD!

DO YOU HAVE ANOTHER SLICE OF PIZZA FOR HER?

GOKURI (GULP)

HEH HEH HEH.

127

128

SFX: MUSHA (CHOMP) MUSHA

IT'S NOT LIKE I'VE GOT TALLER OR MORE MUSCULAR.

MY BODY'S ACTING STRANGE THESE DAYS.

ESPECIALLY BECAUSE STEVE IS RETURNING TO SCHOOL TODAY.

IF ANYONE'S SHARP ENOUGH TO NOTICE, IT'LL BE HIM...

I HAVE TO MAKE SURE PEOPLE DON'T FIND OUT.

THERE'S JUST A FEELING OF RIPPLING STRENGTH THERE NOW.

I CAN TELL MY BODY IS GETTING STRONGER, AND FAST.

I'M TRYING MY BEST TO CONTROL THIS NEW-FOUND STRENGTH, BUT IT'S HARD.

GOTTA BE MORE CARE-FUL...

WAN (WOOF)

YIKES!

PEKO (BOW)

GYU (ZOOM)

OH MY!

...

PAKU PAKU (MUHH)

SFX: CHIRA (PEEK)

DO
(DRIP)

DO

SFX: DOKU (BLUB) DOKU

ZA
(ZSHH)

D-
...DARREN?

DARREN?

H-HEY...

GOKU
(GULP)

GOKU

MY POWER CAME BUBBLING OUT OF ME, AND I WAS SEIZED BY AN UNCONTROLLABLE URGE...

JAAA (FSHHH)

I COULDN'T STOP MYSELF.

...I MIGHT NOT BE ABLE TO REGAIN CONTROL.

THE NEXT TIME SOMETHING LIKE THAT HAPPENS...

YOU WILL COME CRAWLING ON YOUR KNEES BACK TO ME!

CHAPTER 4:
INTO THE NIGHT

AND GOOD-BYE... FOREVER.

FARE-WELL, EVERY-ONE.

TODAY...

...I WILL DIE.

CHAPTER 4:
INTO THE NIGHT

HERE'S DARREN'S FAVOURITE: OVEN-ROASTED CHICKEN!

TA-DAAA!

I JUST HAD A FEELING YOU MIGHT WANT TO HAVE THIS!

CALL IT A MOTHER'S INTUITION.

WOW! WHAT'S THE OCCASION? THIS IS A FEAST!

WELL, WELL! YOU WROTE THAT YOU WANT TO BE LIKE YOUR MOTHER!

YEP!

LOOK, DADDY! I GOT AN A ON MY ESSAY!

WHAT'S THIS? "MY DREAMS FOR THE FUTURE"?

OH, YEAH!

DID YOU SHOW YOUR FATHER YET, ANNIE?

172

178

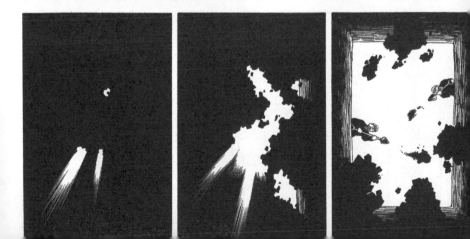

GABAA
(LURCH)

YOU ARE A
BIT GROGGY.
THERE IS A
LITTLE OF THE
POTION STILL
LEFT IN YOU.

ARE
YOU
ALL
RIGHT?

THE POISON
PUTS YOU INTO
A STATE OF
NEAR-DEATH, SO
IT IS NATURAL
THAT YOU ARE
NOT QUITE RIGHT
FOR A WHILE.

MAYBE
THIS WILL
HELP...

......

I FEEL
DEAD
TIRED.

HA
HA.

184

186

STEVE!?

HOW WAS YOUR WAKE-UP CALL...

...VAMPIRE!?

...I CAN'T SUMMON ANY STRENGTH!

OH NO! THE POISON'S STILL ACTIVE...

MMPH!

SFX: BAKI (CRACK)

THE SAGA OF DARREN SHAN ①
Cirque Du Freak

Darren Shan
Takahiro Arai

Translation: Stephen Paul
Lettering: AndWorld Design
Original cover design: Hitoshi SHIRAYAMA + Bay Bridge Studio

Darren Shan Vol. I
Text © 2006 Darren Shan, Artworks © 2006 Takahiro ARAI
All rights reserved
Original Japanese edition published in Japan in 2006
by Shogakukan Inc., Tokyo
Artwork reproduction rights in U.K. and The Commonwealth arranged
with Shogakukan Inc. through Tuttle-Mori Agency, Inc., Tokyo.

English translations © Darren Shan 2009

Published in Great Britain by HarperCollins *Children's Books* 2009
HarperCollins *Children's Books* is a division of HarperCollins *Publishers* Ltd
I London Bridge Street, London SEI 9GF

www.harpercollins.co.uk

ISBN: 978 0 00 732087 5

MIX
Paper from
responsible sources
FSC **FSC® C007454**
www.fsc.org

FSC™ is a non-profit international organisation established to promote the
responsible management of the world's forests. Products carrying the FSC
label are independently certified to assure consumers that they come from
forests that are managed to meet the social, economic and ecological needs
of present and future generations, and other controlled sources.

Find out more about HarperCollins and the environment at
www.harpercollins.co.uk/green

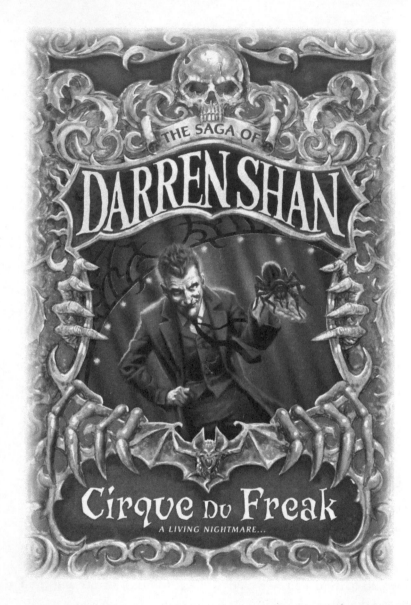

THE SAGA OF

DARREN SHAN

Cirque du Freak

A LIVING NIGHTMARE...

Please flip your book over to enjoy a couple of chapters from
the original novel, also available now!